ELLI WOOLLARD

BENJI DAVIES

The DRAGON and the NIBBLESOME KNIGHT

MACMILLAN CHILDREN'S BOOKS

The Dragons of Dread were a terrible bunch!
They ate boys for their breakfast and girls for their lunch.
But their best things of all, their favourite delights
were dribblesome, nibblesome, knobble-kneed knights.

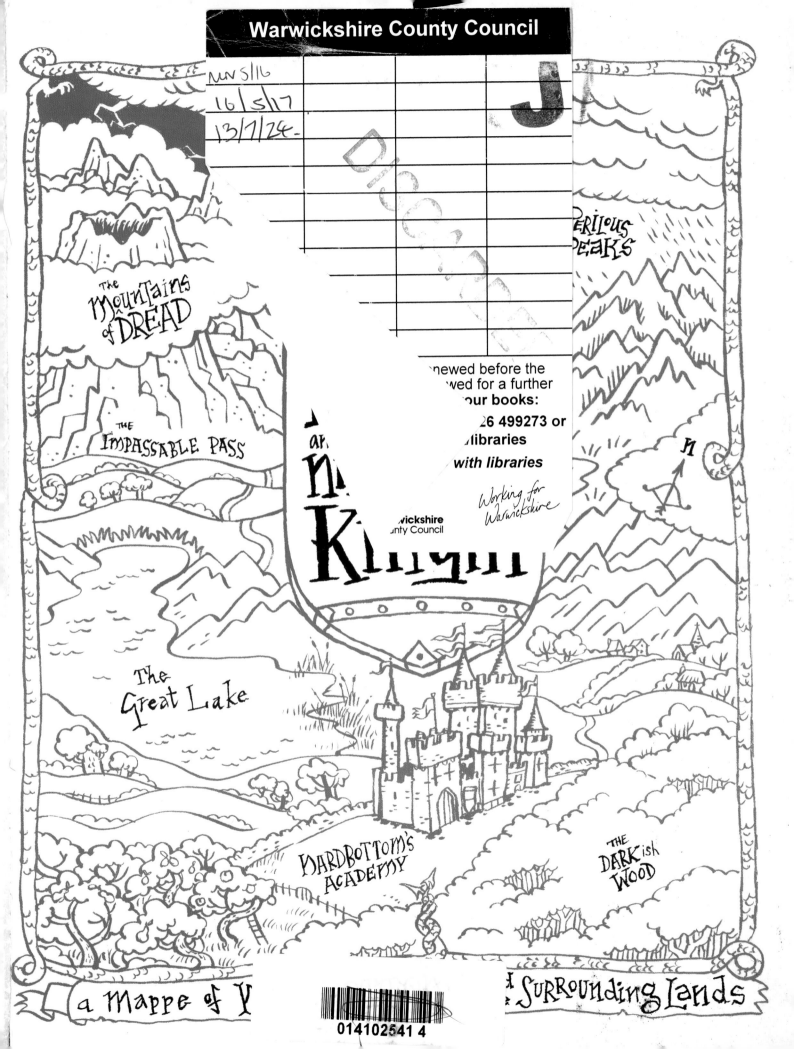

The mountains of DREAD

The IMPASSABLE PASS

PERILOUS PEAKS

The Great Lake

N

HARDBOTTOM'S ACADEMY

The DARKish WOOD

a Mappe of Y   SuRRounding Lands

Prof.

HARDBOTTOM'S
ACADEMY FOR YOUNG KNIGHTS

SCHOOL
SPORTS
DAY!

FIGHT A REAL
LIVE
DRAGON!

TOMORROW

For the Extremely Fantastic
Emily Ford, with thanks
E.W.

For Eleanor
B.D.

First published 2016 by Macmillan Children's Books,
an imprint of Pan Macmillan, 20 New Wharf Road, London N1 9RR.
Associated companies throughout the world. www.panmacmillan.com.
ISBN: 978-1-4472-5480-5 (HB), ISBN: 978-1-4472-5481-2 (PB).
Text © Elli Woollard 2016, Illustrations © Benji Davies 2016, Moral rights asserted.
Printed in Spain   9 8 7 6 5 4 3 2 1

When the smallest of all of the dragons turned four
his parents said, "Dram, you're a baby no more!
This nest's getting cramped and you've never once flown.
Now go bite a nibblesome knight of your own!"

So Dram stretched his wings and he started to flap.

But the lightening went FLASH!

and the thunder went CLAP!

It hailed and it galed and the winds looped and curled.
And they whisked Dram away to the End of the World

Where he thumped and he bumped
and went bounce, clatter, CRASH!

And he fell in a lake
with a fountainous . . .

SPLASH!

Now watching the skies by the edge of the shore

was young James, who had not seen a dragon before.

And he cried, "What was that? It's some rare kind of duck!

It seems to be hurt! What to do? What bad luck!"

So he took off his armour and said with a grin,

"I'm coming to help you!" And he waded right in.

"A lad?" muttered Dram. "Well, he might taste alright.
Though my Mum said I must nab a nibblesome knight."
And he stretched out a claw, then he suddenly stopped.
His leg was all bent and his paw simply flopped.

"Oh duckie!" cried James. "Why, you poor injured thing!
Sit yourself down and I'll make you a sling."

That's better! thought Dram. Now I must find a bite
of a dribblesome, nibblesome, knobble-kneed knight.
So he waved a goodbye and he tried to breathe smoke
but all that came out was a hoarse kind of croak.

"Oh duckie!" cried James, as Dram struggled to roar.

"What a strange sort of quack! Why, your throat must be sore!

Come to the woods and I'll fetch you some honey.

It makes a good medicine, all soothing and runny."

That's better! thought Dram. Now I must find a bite
of a dribblesome, nibblesome, knobble-kneed knight.
So he waved a goodbye and he started to fly
but his wings were too weak to take off in the sky.

"Oh duckie!" cried James. "I'm so dreadfully rude!

You must feel quite faint, let me get you some food.

Come to the orchard, we'll soon fill our tums

full of pears and pink peaches and big purple plums."

"That's better," yawned Dram.

"Now I must find a bite..."

But he fell fast asleep

in the moon-marbled night.

In the morning Dram woke and said, "Hey, I feel fine!
Soon a bite of a nibblesome knight will be mine!"
And he bellowed out billions of billowing flames
then he thought, I'll say bye to that little lad James.

TODAY:
SCHOOL
SPORTS
DAY!
WITH SPECIAL GUESTS
THE DRAGONS OF DREAD

So he strode down the road

and he stomped through the field . . .

. . . and there was young James
with a sword and a shield!

"You're a knight?" shouted Dram.
"You're not simply a lad?"

"You're a dragon?" yelled James.

"You're all beastly and bad?"

"Yes," muttered Dram.

"I suppose I should bite."

"Oh!" mumbled James.

"Then I guess I should fight . . .

. . . it must be all over. The finish.

The end!"

Then they both said at once, "But I can't,
YOU'RE MY FRIEND!"

"My friend!" chortled James,
as he put down his sword.

"My friend!" shouted Dram
and he smiled as he roared.

The knights all said, "Dragons, they're not simply beasts."
The dragons said, "Knights aren't so nice for our feasts."

Nibble at knights? Why, of course we do not!"

Though every so often, they sort of . . .

. . . forgot.

By definition, patterns are regular and repetitive, and their nature can often be enhanced by a symmetrical composition. Shape and form are also important components in abstract compositions, so look to see how they can be exploited. Are there recognizable shapes that work well together? Do you want to include whole shapes, or is there a more interesting composition to be made by closing in further and concentrating on angles and curves?

Colour is another strong element in abstract images. It can be used to draw the viewer's attention to the subject, influence mood and emotional response, and create harmony or disharmony, so try to use colour as part of the composition and look for interesting colour combinations.

REFLECTIONS

Reflections on water make great subjects for abstract studies. Ripples soften the image and distort shapes, making even everyday objects seem unfamiliar. This composition is based on texture, colour and lines. The colours are complementary, creating harmony and the dominant colour is blue, suggesting calm and tranquillity. The strong horizontal lines that run through the image enhance this mood.

Many abstract photographs reveal details that are not visible to the naked eye. This can cause issues with limited depth of field, but this can also be used to further abstract the subject, by placing much of it severely out of focus. If you prefer the whole image in focus, focus stacking (see page 154) is always an option.

DEFINING YOUR STYLE

Trying to develop a personal style can be a daunting task. It is certainly not a short process, nor is it an easy one, and it requires a fair amount of introspection. The factors that shape our style are the various choices that we make as photographers, including subject, the equipment we use, the lighting we favour and how we process our images. The obvious starting point on the road to developing your own style is to examine the factors that can contribute to a personal style and then analyzing how these influence your work.

SUBJECT

To some extent, this is independent of style, as your personal style can theoretically be applied to any subject. However, we are all drawn to certain subjects more strongly than others, whether it's trees, streams or waves crashing on the shore. What attracts us is related to our personality and how we see the world, so it's worth identifying the subjects that most strongly motivate you to pick up a camera.

EQUIPMENT AND MEDIUM

Whether you favour film or digital, 35mm, medium format, large format, colour or black and white influences the 'look' of your images. Your choice of format is part of your personal style: do you tend to shoot in horizontal or vertical orientation? Do you like panoramic or squarer formats?

Lens choice also has a big influence. Wide-angle lenses allow greater depth of field and the possibility to create an exaggerated perspective, whereas longer focal lengths create a compressed, 'stacked' look that can be useful for compositions based around layers. Whether you use primes or zooms will also affect the way you work: zooms allow very precise framing from your chosen viewpoint, whereas primes require you to move to frame the shot how you want, which may compromise viewpoint. On the other hand, primes are generally sharper and resolve more detail than zooms, although this is certainly not a universal truth – there are some excellent zoom lenses available. Individual lenses will also have variations in how they handle colour and contrast and how much distortion they have, all of which will affect the look of your images.

LIGHTING

Most landscape photographers prefer shooting in the golden hours, but there is no rule that says you have to restrict yourself to this type of lighting and there are those whose work is recognisable precisely because they favour overcast, diffused light in the middle of the day or shooting long exposures in extremely low light, for example. Direction of light is also closely related to style: do you prefer sidelit, backlit or front-lit subjects?

EXPOSURE

Exposure is a powerful tool for creative expression. High-key and low-key images have a completely different mood, and with certain subjects your choice of shutter speed can also affect the atmosphere; extremely long exposures give an ethereal look to some scenes, whereas shorter exposures can produce images that appear more powerful and dynamic.

YOUR PERSONAL STYLE
Subject, choice of equipment, use of foreground, line, shape and perspective, how you treat colour and how you expose your images are just some of the factors that contribute to your personal style.

173

APPROACH

This relates to how much planning you do. Some photographers research their locations meticulously, checking the angle of the sun and so forth, to make sure they visit the location in what they consider to be the 'best' light (or at least their favoured type of lighting). They will set up in advance and wait for the right conditions, perhaps making multiple visits to the same location. Once they've found their composition, they may only make slight adjustments. This will mean they won't get a huge variety of images, but they will get the one that they want.

Others photographers prefer to be more spontaneous and react to what they find in front of them. They are more reactive, and will hunt for the best light; if it's not happening where they are, they'll move on and see if there's something better elsewhere.

SUBJECT CHOICE AND EXPOSURE

All photographers find themselves drawn to certain types of subject, which can help to identify their personal style. In this case, the isolated object (often man-made, or at least very structural in nature) in an expanse of empty space is a typical choice of the author. An exposure time of 4 seconds, timed to capture the backwash of a wave, creates strong texture in the foreground, something else that typifies the author's work.

Once they feel they've nailed a shot, they'll move on to try something different. This type of photographer is likely to get a greater variety of shots, but runs the risk of missing the best combination of light and composition. However, both approaches are equally valid, and both are strongly related to personality – which are you? You may find you combine elements of each.

FRAMING

Framing and composition are the most important factors in determining personal style, so it's worth looking at how you frame your images and asking yourself the following questions: Do you prefer a wide view or do you prefer to highlight details within the scene? Do you go for extensive depth of field? How do you treat perspective? This relates strongly to lens choice, but there are other factors as well – for example, do you like to show depth through foreground interest or the use of guiding lines? Do you favour the 'big' foreground or something subtler? Where do you like to place foreground interest – centred or to one side? How do you divide the frame – following the rule of thirds, or something else? How do you treat shape, line and form? Do you go for a 'classical' composition or something different? Which colours do you favour? Do you

FRAMING AND LIGHT
Your choice of framing and your preferred lighting help to identify your individual style. Here, the frame is divided very traditionally, close to the rule of thirds, with strong foreground interest. The shot is also characterized by low sidelighting, which reveals texture and gives volume and depth to the castle.

prefer complementary colours? How much colour saturation? What sort of mood do you like to convey in your compositions? How do you treat movement?

POST-PROCESSING

Another way of putting your own stamp on your photography is via post-processing, and your personal look can include how much colour saturation you apply, how much contrast, how warm or cool your images are and the amount of sharpening and clarity you prefer.

ANALYZING THE AUTHOR'S PERSONAL STYLE:
MARK BAUER

Having identified the factors that define a personal style, the logical step is to use this to analyze your own images and identify the essence of your style. From there you are in a position to develop your personal style further. To demonstrate this process, we've analyzed our own styles.

SUBJECT

Any landscapes with big vistas, but Mark is especially drawn to water and seascapes in particular, spending a lot of time near the coast in Dorset, UK.

EQUIPMENT AND MEDIUM

Mark cut his teeth on 6 x 7cm medium-format cameras and that continues to influence his work. He now uses a full-frame digital SLR, shooting primarily with wide-angle zooms, but still prefers a squarer aspect ratio to the 3:2 of his sensor.

LIGHTING

The majority of Mark's pictures are taken in the golden hours, but he also favours twilight and pre-dawn light. He will use midday light on overcast days for black and white and long exposure work, and prefers sidelighting and backlighting to frontal lighting.

EXPOSURE

Texture is an important part of Mark's compositions, so he likes long exposures that capture movement in water and soften skies. Although a number of shots feature ultra-long exposures to simplify compositional elements, he generally prefers moderate exposure times of 2–20 seconds, as this results in a more textured look and can be used to create lines in foregrounds.

APPROACH

Mark is very much a planner, spending a lot of time looking at weather forecasts and checking sunrise and sunset angles. On location, once he's found a composition he will often not change much, just continuing to tweak it slightly until he's absolutely satisfied it can't be improved further. Then it's a case of waiting for the light to be right.

FRAMING

Mark generally favours a traditional style of composition, with a strong minimalist influence. He likes extensive depth of field and strong perspective effects, but favours guiding lines and curves rather than a 'big foreground' approach. Compositions are very 'structured', often featuring architectural elements in them and Mark often tries to convey a tranquil, romantic mood.

POST-PROCESSING

Processing will quite often involve a change of aspect ratio, and having spent several years shooting with Fuji Velvia, Mark likes saturated, punchy colours, and images with strong contrast.

MARK'S PERSONAL STYLE
This shot of a bridge crossing a river in Dorset in the UK illustrates many of the characteristics of Mark's personal style. Shot on 6 x 7cm Velvia in the romantic light of a misty dawn, it is a very 'structural' composition, with strong lines creating a powerful sense of perspective through to a vanishing point. There is strong colour saturation and there is an overall mood of tranquillity.

ANALYZING THE AUTHOR'S PERSONAL STYLE:

ROSS HODDINOTT

SUBJECT

Ross's landscapes are a mixture of wide views and more detailed shots. He is a macro specialist and this is reflected in the way he is attracted to details in the landscape. He grew up near the coast, so it is no surprise that water plays a large part in many of his compositions.

EQUIPMENT AND MEDIUM

Ross worked for many years with 35mm transparency film and was an early adopter of digital cameras. He now shoots with a full-frame digital SLR, almost exclusively in colour, and is very comfortable with the flexibility that the 3:2 aspect ratio offers.

LIGHTING

Ross's preference is for sidelighting during the golden hours, but he also works a lot in twilight and pre-dawn. He is not averse to working in what might be thought of as 'poor' light, believing that as long as there is some texture in the sky, there is the possibility of making good images.

EXPOSURE

Ross's exposures are often dominated by light tones, with soft contrast, but he is also happy to let blacks record as pure black and likes to emphasize form with silhouettes. When photographing water he will often use a shutter speed that will create or highlight the texture of breaking waves, waterfalls, and so on, but will occasionally use ultra-long exposures to smooth out surfaces and simplify compositions.

APPROACH

Careful planning is evident is Ross's work, and he spends time researching tides, weather forecasts, sunrise and sunset angles in order to choose the best time to visit locations. However, on location he is happy to be flexible and react to conditions, often taking a wide variety of compositions.

FRAMING

Ross's compositions follow a classical balance. He leans towards simplicity (though rarely minimalism), with extensive depth of field, strong foregrounds, clean lines and bold shapes. Details and textures are often prominent.

POST-PROCESSING

Ross aims for a 'natural' look with his processing, generally processing his images less aggressively than co-author Mark Bauer, and with slightly less contrast. He doesn't like an overly warm white balance, preferring coolish tones.

ROSS'S PERSONAL STYLE
A simple, balanced composition and the naturally cool tones of twilight mark this as one of Ross's images, taken in Slovakia. The classical division of the frame into thirds gives the picture a sense of harmony, and there is a clear focal point in the background. The strong foreground helps to convey a feeling of depth, with the blue hues, mist and smooth water create a sense of tranquillity.

TECHNICAL DETAILS

9 MISTY RIVER
Camera: Canon EOS 5D Mk II
Lens: 70–200mm (at 163mm)
Aperture: f/11
Shutter speed: 6 sec.
ISO: 100
Filter(s): 4-stop ND

25 LONG EXPOSURE
Camera: Nikon D800
Lens: 17–35mm (at 19mm)
Aperture: f/11
Shutter speed: 60 sec.
ISO: 100
Filter(s): 10-stop ND, 2-stop ND grad

40 THE BEST APERTURE
Camera: Nikon D700
Lens: 70–200mm (at 125mm)
Aperture: f/4
Shutter speed: 1/40 sec.
ISO: 200
Filter(s): –

10 TECHNICAL ACCURACY
Camera: Nikon D800E
Lens: 16–35mm (at 35mm)
Aperture: f/16
Shutter speed: 0.8 sec.
ISO: 100
Filter(s): 2-stop ND grad

27 GRADUATED ND COMPARISON
Camera: Nikon D800E
Lens: 16–35mm (at 22mm)
Aperture: f/16
Shutter speed: 5 sec.
ISO: 100
Filter(s): 2-stop ND grad (filtered)

43 DEPTH OF FIELD CALCULATOR
Camera: Nikon D800E
Lens: 16–35mm (at 22mm)
Aperture: f/16
Shutter speed: 20 sec
ISO: 100
Filter(s): 0.6 ND grad, 0.9 ND

13 ASPECT RATIO
Camera: Nikon D800E
Lens: 16–35mm (at 18mm)
Aperture: f/16
Shutter speed: 1.3 sec.
ISO: 100
Filter(s): 2-stop ND

28 REFLECTIONS
Camera: Nikon D800
Lens: 24–70mm (at 27mm)
Aperture: f/16
Shutter speed: 5 sec.
ISO: 100
Filter(s): Polarizer

45 HYPERFOCAL DISTANCE
Camera: Nikon D800
Lens: 24–70mm (at 32mm)
Aperture: f/16
Shutter speed: 30 sec.
ISO: 100
Filter(s): 3-stop ND, 2-stop ND grad

15 FULL-FRAME DIGITAL
Camera: Nikon D800
Lens: 24–70mm (at 31mm)
Aperture: f/11
Shutter speed: 30 sec.
ISO: 100
Filter(s): 2-stop ND grad

30 LEVELLING AID
Camera: Nikon D800E
Lens: 16–35mm (at 16mm)
Aperture: f/14
Shutter speed: 6 sec.
ISO: 100
Filter(s): 2-stop ND grad

47 STARBURST EFFECT
Camera: Nikon D700
Lens: 17–35mm (at 17mm)
Aperture: f/22
Shutter speed: 10 sec.
ISO: 200
Filter(s): 3-stop ND, 3-stop ND grad

17 WIDE-ANGLE LENS
Camera: Nikon D300
Lens: 10–24mm (at 20mm)
Aperture: f/16
Shutter speed: 180 sec.
ISO: 100
Filter(s): 10-stop ND, 3-stop ND grad, polarizer

32 CREATIVE CONTROL
Camera: Nikon D800E
Lens: 16–35mm (at 22mm)
Aperture: f/11
Shutter speed: 180 sec.
ISO: 200
Filter(s): 3-stop ND, 2-stop ND grad

49 COLOUR DOMINANCE
Camera: Nikon D700
Lens: 17–35mm (at 17mm)
Aperture: f/11
Shutter speed: 1/20 sec.
ISO: 400
Filter(s): Polarizer

18 STANDARD FOCAL LENGTH
Camera: Nikon D800
Lens: 50mm
Aperture: f/16
Shutter speed: 0.4 sec.
ISO: 100
Filter(s): 2-stop ND grad

35 ADJUSTING EXPOSURE
Camera: Nikon D800E
Lens: 16–35mm (at 18mm)
Aperture: f/11
Shutter speed: 10 sec.
ISO: 200
Filter(s): 2-stop ND grad

50 DIFFUSED DETAIL
Camera: Nikon D800
Lens: 70–200mm (at 122mm)
Aperture: f/11
Shutter speed: 50 sec.
ISO: 200
Filter(s): –

19 SIMPLICITY WORKS
Camera: Nikon D800E
Lens: 70–200mm (at 110mm)
Aperture: f/11
Shutter speed: 1/100 sec.
ISO: 100
Filter(s): –

36 THE 'CORRECT' EXPOSURE
Camera: Nikon D800
Lens: 24–70mm (at 45mm)
Aperture: f/11
Shutter speed: 30 sec.
ISO: 100
Filter(s): 3-stop ND, 2-stop ND grad

51 CREATIVE WHITE BALANCE
Camera: Nikon D800E
Lens: 16–35mm (at 16mm)
Aperture: f/11
Shutter speed: 4 sec.
ISO: 400
Filter(s): 2-stop ND grad

21 STABILITY
Camera: Nikon D700
Lens: 24–70mm (at 56mm)
Aperture: f/11
Shutter speed: 60 sec.
ISO: 200
Filter(s): 2-stop ND grad

39 VISUAL IMPACT
Camera: Nikon D300
Lens: 10–24mm (at 10mm)
Aperture: f/20
Shutter speed: 30 sec.
ISO: 100
Filter(s): 3-stop ND grad

52 VISUAL BALANCE
Camera: Canon EOS 5D Mk III
Lens: 24–105mm (at 40mm)
Aperture: f/16
Shutter speed: 1/20 sec.
ISO: 100
Filter(s): 3-stop ND grad

55 BALANCING CONTRASTING POINTS
Camera: Canon EOS 5D Mk III
Lens: 16–35mm (at 16mm)
Aperture: f/22
Shutter speed: 0.8 sec.
ISO: 100
Filter(s): 3-stop ND grad

55 IMPLIED MOVEMENT FOR BALANCE
Camera: Canon EOS 5D Mk II
Lens: 16–35mm (at 16mm)
Aperture: f/16
Shutter speed: 30 sec.
ISO: 100
Filter(s): 4-stop ND, 2-stop ND grad

56 A SINGLE SUBJECT
Camera: Fuji X-E1
Lens: 18–55mm (at 27mm)
Aperture: f/16
Shutter speed: 58 sec.
ISO: 200
Filter(s): 6-stop ND

57 PLACING A MOVING SUBJECT
Camera: Canon EOS 5D Mk III
Lens: 24–105mm (at 60mm)
Aperture: f/11
Shutter speed: 1/20 sec.
ISO: 800
Filter(s): –

58 THE RULE OF THIRDS
Camera: Canon EOS 5D Mk II
Lens: 17–40mm (at 28mm)
Aperture: f/16
Shutter speed: 1.3 sec.
ISO: 100
Filter(s): Polarizer

59 BREAKING THE RULE OF THIRDS
Camera: Canon EOS 5D Mk III
Lens: 21mm
Aperture: f/22
Shutter speed: 6 sec.
ISO: 100
Filter(s): 3-stop ND, 3-stop ND grad

61 GOLDEN SECTION IN PRACTICE
Camera: Canon EOS 5D Mk II
Lens: 24–105mm (at 35mm)
Aperture: f/11
Shutter speed: 1/50 sec.
ISO: 100
Filter(s): 2-stop ND grad, polarizer

63 FIT THE GOLDEN SECTION
Camera: Canon EOS 5D Mk III
Lens: 16–35mm (at 16mm)
Aperture: f/11
Shutter speed: 13 sec.
ISO: 200
Filter(s): 3-stop ND, 2-stop ND grad

65 THE GOLDEN SPIRAL IN PRACTICE
Camera: Canon EOS 5D Mk III
Lens: 16–35mm (at 20mm)
Aperture: f/16
Shutter speed: 6 sec. (second exposure of 0.8 sec. for sky)
ISO: 100
Filter(s): 3-stop ND

65 A GOLDEN TRIANGLE GRID
Camera: Canon EOS 5D Mk III
Lens: 16–35mm (at 21mm)
Aperture: f/16
Shutter speed: 30 sec.
ISO: 100
Filter(s): 4-stop ND, 3-stop ND grad

67 NEAR SYMMETRY
Camera: Canon EOS 5D Mk III
Lens: 17–40mm (at 19mm)
Aperture: f/16
Shutter speed: 24 sec.
ISO: 100
Filter(s): 3-stop ND, 3-stop ND grad

67 REFLECTIONS
Camera: Canon EOS 5D Mk III
Lens: 16–35mm (at 29mm)
Aperture: f/16
Shutter speed: 3.2 sec.
ISO: 100
Filter(s): –

68 THREE – THE MAGIC NUMBER
Camera: Canon EOS 1Ds Mk II
Lens: 24–105mm (at 35mm)
Aperture: f/16
Shutter speed: 1/4 sec.
ISO: 100
Filter(s): 3-stop ND grad

69 BREAKING THE RULE?
Camera: Canon EOS 5D Mk III
Lens: 24–105mm (at 24mm)
Aperture: f/16
Shutter speed: 6 sec.
ISO: 200
Filter(s): 4-stop ND filter, polarizer

70 VERTICAL MOVEMENT
Camera: Canon EOS 5D Mk II
Lens: 21mm
Aperture: f/14
Shutter speed: 20 sec.
ISO: 100
Filter(s): 3-stop ND, 3-stop ND grad

71 LANDSCAPE OR PORTRAIT?
Camera: Canon EOS 5D Mk II
Lens: 17–40mm (at 20mm)
Aperture: f/16
Shutter speed: 0.5 sec.
ISO: 100
Filter(s): 3-stop ND grad

72 A SENSE OF DEPTH
Camera: Canon EOS 5D Mk II
Lens: 17–40mm (at 17mm)
Aperture: f/16
Shutter speed: 15 sec.
ISO: 100
Filter(s): 4-stop ND, 2-stop ND

74 WIDE-ANGLE PERSPECTIVE
Camera: Canon EOS 5D Mk II
Lens: 17–40mm (at 17mm)
Aperture: f/22
Shutter speed: 5 sec.
ISO: 100
Filter(s): –

75 TELEPHOTO COMPRESSION
Camera: Canon EOS 5D Mk II
Lens: 24–105mm (at 80mm)
Aperture: f/11
Shutter speed: 1/8 sec.
ISO: 100
Filter(s): 3-stop ND grad

76 FINDING A VANISHING POINT
Camera: Nikon D800E
Lens: 16–35mm (at 24mm)
Aperture: f/11
Shutter speed: 6 sec.
ISO: 100
Filter(s): 2-stop ND, polarizer

77 HIGHLIGHTING THE FOCAL POINT
Camera: Canon EOS 5D Mk II
Lens: 17–40mm (at 17mm)
Aperture: f/16
Shutter speed: 4 sec.
ISO: 100
Filter(s): 3-stop ND grad

77 CONVERGING LINES
Camera: Canon EOS 5D Mk II
Lens: 18mm
Aperture: f/16
Shutter speed: 40 sec.
ISO: 100
Filter(s): 4-stop ND, 3-stop ND grad

78 LOW VIEWPOINT
Camera: Canon EOS 5D Mk II
Lens: 21mm
Aperture: f/16
Shutter speed: 30 sec.
ISO: 100
Filter(s): 4-stop ND, 2-stop ND grad

79 THE 'BIG ROCK' FOREGROUND
Camera: Canon EOS 1Ds Mk II
Lens: 17–40mm (at 20mm)
Aperture: f/20
Shutter speed: 1.3 sec.
ISO: 100
Filter(s): 3-stop ND grad

80 THE SMALL FOREGROUND
Camera: Canon EOS 5D
Lens: 17–40mm (at 17mm)
Aperture: f/22
Shutter speed: 1/10 sec.
ISO: 100
Filter(s): 3-stop ND grad

81 CONVEYING DEPTH
Camera: Hasselblad H5D-40
Lens: 35–90mm (at 35mm)
Aperture: f/16
Shutter speed: 5 sec.
ISO: 100
Filter(s): –

81 EMPTY FOREGROUND
Camera: Canon EOS 5D Mk II
Lens: 24–105mm (at 28mm)
Aperture: f/22
Shutter speed: 4 sec.
ISO: 100
Filter(s): 4-stop ND, polarizer

83 SHARP FOREGROUND DETAIL
Camera: Canon EOS 5D Mk III
Lens: 24mm TS-E
Aperture: f/8
Shutter speed: 6 sec.
ISO: 100
Filter(s): 4-stop ND filter

84 FRONT-TO-BACK SHARPNESS (1)
Camera: Canon EOS 5D Mk II
Lens: 24mm TS-E
Aperture: f/8
Shutter speed: 1/8 sec.
ISO: 100
Filter(s): Polarizer

85 FRONT-TO-BACK SHARPNESS (2)
Camera: Canon EOS 5D Mk II
Lens: 24mm TS-E
Aperture: f/8
Shutter speed: 1/8 sec.
ISO: 100
Filter(s): Polarizer

86 VOLUME PERSPECTIVE
Camera: Canon EOS 5D Mk II
Lens: 16–35mm (at 16mm)
Aperture: f/11
Shutter speed: 1/13 sec.
ISO: 100
Filter(s): 3-stop ND grad

87 AERIAL PERSPECTIVE
Camera: Canon EOS 5D
Lens: 70–200mm (at 90mm)
Aperture: f/11
Shutter speed: 1/60 sec.
ISO: 100
Filter(s): 2-stop ND grad

87 COLOUR PERSPECTIVE
Camera: Canon EOS 5D Mk II
Lens: 24–105mm (at 24mm)
Aperture: f/16
Shutter speed: 1/8 sec.
ISO: 400
Filter(s): 2-stop ND grad

88 VISUAL SEPARATION
Camera: Canon EOS 5D Mk III
Lens: 18mm
Aperture: f/11
Shutter speed: 301 sec.
ISO: 200
Filter(s): 10-stop ND, 2-stop ND grad

89 LOW VIEWPOINT (1)
Camera: Canon EOS 1Ds Mk II
Lens: 17–40mm (at 20mm)
Aperture: f/16
Shutter speed: 1/2 sec.
ISO: 100
Filter(s): 2-stop ND grad, polarizer

89 LOW VIEWPOINT (2)
Camera: Canon EOS 1Ds Mk II
Lens: 17–40mm (at 20mm)
Aperture: f/16
Shutter speed: 1/5 sec.
ISO: 100
Filter(s): 2-stop ND grad, polarizer

90 A SENSE OF SCALE
Camera: Canon EOS 5D Mk III
Lens: 24–105mm (at 24mm)
Aperture: f/11
Shutter speed: 1/3 sec.
ISO: 100
Filter(s): 2-stop ND grad

91 FRAMES WITHIN THE FRAME
Camera: Pentax 67II
Lens: 105mm
Aperture: f/22
Shutter speed: 1/8 sec.
ISO: 50 (Fuji Velvia film)
Filter(s): –

92 GEOMETRY IN THE LANDSCAPE
Camera: Canon EOS 5D Mk II
Lens: 21mm
Aperture: f/11
Shutter speed: 50 sec.
ISO: 100
Filter(s): 2-stop ND grad

94 LINES AS SUBJECT
Camera: Canon EOS 5D Mk II
Lens: 24–105mm (at 24mm)
Aperture: f/11
Shutter speed: 437 sec.
ISO: 400
Filter(s): 10-stop ND, 2-stop ND grad

95 LEADING THE EYE
Camera: Pentax 67II
Lens: 45mm
Aperture: f/16
Shutter speed: Unrecorded
ISO: 50 (Fuji Velvia film)
Filter(s): 3-stop ND grad

97 EQUILIBRIUM
Camera: Canon EOS 5D Mk II
Lens: 21mm
Aperture: f/16
Shutter speed: 1/5 sec. (shot 1), 1/25 sec. (shot 2); images blended
ISO: 100
Filter(s): –

97 ARCS
Camera: Canon EOS 5D Mk II
Lens: 24–105mm (at 28mm)
Aperture: f/11
Shutter speed: 311 sec.
ISO: 200
Filter(s): 10-stop ND, 2-stop ND grad

98 EXPOSURE TIME
Camera: Canon EOS 5D Mk II
Lens: 21mm
Aperture: f/22
Shutter speed: 46 sec.
ISO: 100
Filter(s): 4-stop ND, 3-stop ND grad

99 POINTING IN
Camera: Canon EOS 5D Mk III
Lens: 18mm
Aperture: f/16
Shutter speed: 10 sec.
ISO: 100
Filter(s): 2-stop ND grad

101 TRIANGULAR ARRANGEMENT
Camera: Canon EOS 5D Mk III
Lens: 16–35mm (at 21mm)
Aperture: f/16
Shutter speed: 10 sec.
ISO: 100
Filter(s): 2-stop ND grad

101 IMPLIED TRIANGLE
Camera: Canon EOS 5D Mk II
Lens: 18mm
Aperture: f/16
Shutter speed: 1/20 sec.
ISO: 100
Filter(s): 2-stop ND grad.

102 SEPARATE PLANES
Camera: Canon EOS 5D Mk II
Lens: 70–200mm (at 200mm)
Aperture: f/16
Shutter speed: 0.4 sec.
ISO: 100
Filter(s): –

103 FOREGROUND PLANE
Camera: Canon EOS 5D
Lens: 17–40mm (at 21mm)
Aperture: f/14
Shutter speed: 1/8 sec.
ISO: 400
Filter(s): 2-stop ND grad

105 LEADING THE EYE IN
Camera: Canon EOS 5D Mk II
Lens: 21mm
Aperture: f/11
Shutter speed: 363 sec.
ISO: 200
Filter(s): 2-stop ND grad

105 FOLLOWING A WATER FLOW
Camera: Canon EOS 6D
Lens: 17–40mm (at 17mm)
Aperture: f/16
Shutter speed: 3.2 sec.
ISO: 100
Filter(s): 4-stop ND

107 WATER BLUR
Camera: Nikon D700
Lens: 17–35mm (at 20mm)
Aperture: f/16
Shutter speed:
ISO: 200
Filter(s): 3-stop ND

107 MOTION IN CROPS
Camera: Nikon D800
Lens: 17–35mm (at 20mm)
Aperture: f/16
Shutter speed: 1.3 sec.
ISO: 100
Filter(s): 3-stop ND

108 GOLDEN ARCH
Camera: Canon EOS 5D Mk III
Lens: 16–35mm (at 21mm)
Aperture: f/11
Shutter speed: 2.5 sec.
ISO: 125
Filter(s): 3-stop ND, polarizer

110 REVEALING TEXTURE
Camera: Canon EOS 5D Mk II
Lens: 24–105mm (at 24mm)
Aperture: f/16
Shutter speed: 80 sec.
ISO: 100
Filter(s): 10-stop ND

111 LOW FRONT LIGHTING
Camera: Canon EOS 5D Mk II
Lens: 21mm
Aperture: f/11
Shutter speed: 170 sec.
ISO: 100
Filter(s): 10-stop ND, 2-stop ND grad

111 LAYERED SIDE LIGHTING
Camera: Canon EOS 1Ds Mk II
Lens: 24–105mm (at 55mm)
Aperture: f/16
Shutter speed: 1 sec.
ISO: 100
Filter(s): 2-stop ND grad

112 THE GOLDEN HOUR
Camera: Canon EOS 5D Mk III
Lens: 21mm
Aperture: f/20
Shutter speed: 5 sec. (main exposure)
ISO: 100
Filter(s): 3-stop ND grad

113 THE BLUE HOUR
Camera: Canon EOS 5D Mk II
Lens: 21mm
Aperture: f/11
Shutter speed: 479 sec.
ISO: 200
Filter(s): –

115 SUMMER COLOURS
Camera: Canon EOS 5D Mk II
Lens: 18mm
Aperture: f/16
Shutter speed: 2.5 sec.
ISO: 100
Filter(s): 3-stop ND, polarizer

115 AUTUMN MIST
Camera: Canon EOS 5D Mk II
Lens: 24–105mm (at 105mm)
Aperture: f/11
Shutter speed: 1/125 sec.
ISO: 100
Filter(s): –

116 LONG EXPOSURE SEASCAPE
Camera: Canon EOS 5D Mk II
Lens: 17–40mm (at 17mm)
Aperture: f/11
Shutter speed: 13 sec.
ISO: 200
Filter(s): –

117 MINIMALIST SNOW SCENE
Camera: Canon EOS 5D Mk II
Lens: 24–105mm (at 105mm)
Aperture: f/11
Shutter speed: 1/20 sec.
ISO: 100
Filter(s): Polarizer

119 LOW LIGHT COLOUR
Camera: Canon EOS 5D Mk II
Lens: 21mm
Aperture: f/16
Shutter speed: 120 sec.
ISO: 100
Filter(s): 2-stop ND grad

120 CURVED LIGHT
Camera: Canon EOS 5D Mk II
Lens: 21mm
Aperture: f/2.8
Shutter speed: 15 sec.
ISO: 3200
Filter(s): –

121 CONVERGING LINES
Camera: Canon EOS 5D Mark III
Lens: 16–35mm at 16mm
Aperture: f/2.8
Shutter speed: 15 sec.
ISO: 1600
Filter(s): 2-stop ND grad

123 TEXTURED SKY
Camera: Fuji X-E1
Lens: 18–55mm (at 18mm)
Aperture: f/11
Shutter speed: 125 sec.
ISO: 200
Filter(s): 10-stop ND, polarizer

123 BAD WEATHER MONO
Camera: Canon EOS 5D Mk II
Lens: 17–40mm (at 17mm)
Aperture: f/16
Shutter speed: 302 sec.
ISO: 100
Filter(s): 10-stop ND

124 SILHOUETTED WINDMILL
Camera: Canon EOS 5D Mk II
Lens: 70–200mm (at 200mm)
Aperture: f/11
Shutter speed: 300 sec.
ISO: 100
Filter(s): 4-stop ND

125 SILHOUETTED TREE
Camera: Nikon D700
Lens: 70–200mm (at 100mm)
Aperture: f/11
Shutter speed: 1/30 sec.
ISO: 200
Filter(s): –

126 CASTLE AT SUNSET
Camera: Canon EOS 5D Mk III
Lens: 16–35mm (at 25mm)
Aperture: f/16
Shutter speed: 1/2 sec.
ISO: 100
Filter(s): 2-stop ND grad

127 SPOTLIT ROCKS
Camera: Canon EOS 5D Mk II
Lens: 17–40mm (at 19mm)
Aperture: f/16
Shutter speed: 1/8 sec.
ISO: 100
Filter(s): Polarizer

128 THE ESSENCE OF A VIEW
Camera: Nikon D800E
Lens: 16–35mm (at 18mm)
Aperture: f/14
Shutter speed: 8 sec.
ISO: 100
Filter(s): 2-stop ND grad

131 THE CLIFFTOP VIEW
Camera: Nikon D700
Lens: 17–35mm (at 19mm)
Aperture: f/13
Shutter speed: 30 sec.
ISO: 100
Filter(s): 2-stop ND grad

133 LOW VIEWPOINTS
Camera: Nikon D800
Lens: 17–35mm (at 19mm)
Aperture: f/16
Shutter speed: 10 sec.
ISO: 100
Filter(s): 2-stop ND grad

133 CAPTURING WATER TRAILS
Camera: Nikon D800
Lens: 16–35mm (at 22mm)
Aperture: f/16
Shutter speed: 0.8 sec.
ISO: 100
Filter(s): 2-stop ND grad

135 LIGHT AND DARK CONTRAST
Camera: Nikon D800E
Lens: 16–35mm (at 26mm)
Aperture: f/16
Shutter speed: 1/4 sec.
ISO: 100
Filter(s): 2-stop ND grad, polarizer

135 SAFETY AS A PRIORITY
Camera: Nikon D800E
Lens: 16–35mm (at 18mm)
Aperture: f/11
Shutter speed: 1/5 sec.
ISO: 100
Filter(s): 2-stop ND grad, polarizer

137 WOODLAND MIST
Camera: Nikon D700
Lens: 24–70mm (at 70mm)
Aperture: f/11
Shutter speed: 2 sec.
ISO: 200
Filter(s): –

139 FRAME WATERFALLS
Camera: Nikon D800E
Lens: 24–70mm (at 42mm)
Aperture: f/8
Shutter speed: 3 sec.
ISO: 200
Filter(s): Polarizer

139 CAREFUL EXPOSURE
Camera: Nikon D700
Lens: 17–35mm (at 19mm)
Aperture: f/18
Shutter speed: 1.3 sec.
ISO: 100
Filter(s): Polarizer

141 SYMMETRY
Camera: Nikon D800
Lens: 24–70mm (at 24mm)
Aperture: f/11
Shutter speed: 8 sec.
ISO: 100
Filter(s): 2-stop ND grad

141 REEDS AND REFLECTION
Camera: Nikon D700
Lens: 17–35mm (at 24mm)
Aperture: f/11
Shutter speed: 30 sec.
ISO: 200
Filter(s): 2-stop ND grad, polarizer

142 PEBBLE
Camera: Nikon D800
Lens: 105mm macro
Aperture: f/14
Shutter speed: 0.8 sec.
ISO: 100
Filter(s): –

143 ICE
Camera: Nikon D300
Lens: 105mm macro
Aperture: f/11
Shutter speed: 1/20 sec.
ISO: 200
Filter(s): –

144 ICE BEACH
Camera: Canon EOS 5D Mk III
Lens: 16–35mm (at 18mm)
Aperture: f/16
Shutter speed: 4 sec.
ISO: 200
Filter(s): 3-stop ND, 3-stop ND grad, polarizer

148 MOUNTAINS
Camera: Canon EOS 5D Mk III
Lens: 24–105mm (at 80mm)
Aperture: f/16
Shutter speed: 1/5 sec.
ISO: 100
Filter(s): –

149 LAKE REFLECTIONS
Camera: Canon EOS 5D Mk III
Lens: 24–105mm (at 35mm)
Aperture: f/16
Shutter speed: 90 sec.
ISO: 100
Filter(s): 10-stop ND

151 CREATIVE SHARPENING
Camera: Canon EOS 5D Mk III
Lens: 21mm
Aperture: f/22
Shutter speed: 10 sec.
ISO: 100
Filter(s): 2-stop ND grad

153 LOCAL ENHANCEMENTS
Camera: Canon EOS 5D Mk III
Lens: 70–200mm at 98mm
Aperture: f/8
Shutter speed: 0.5 sec.
ISO: 100
Filter(s): –

155 FOCUS STACKING
Camera: Canon EOS 5D Mk III
Lens: 16–35mm at 29mm
Aperture: f/8
Shutter speed: 8 sec.
ISO: 100
Filter(s): 4-stop ND filter

157 PANORAMIC STITCHIING
Camera: Canon 5D mark II
Lens: 17–40mm at 17mm
Aperture: f/13
Shutter speed: 1/25th secondy
ISO: 100
Filter(s): –

159 EXPOSURE BLENDING
Camera: Canon EOS 5D Mk III
Lens: 16–35mm at 20mm
Aperture: f/16
Shutter speed: 2 sec. on sky
15 sec. on foreground
ISO: 100
Filter(s): 4-stop ND filter

161 CONVERTING TO BLACK & WHITE
Camera: Canon 5D mark IIII
Lens: 170–200mm at 140mm
Aperture: f/9
Shutter speed: 1/125th sec
ISO: 100
Filter(s): polariser

162 ICELANDIC SUNSET
Camera: Canon EOS 5D Mk III
Lens: 24–105mm (at 58mm)
Aperture: f/16
Shutter speed: 5 sec.
ISO: 100
Filter(s): 3-stop ND, 2-stop ND grad

164 CLASSICAL COMPOSITION
Camera: Canon EOS 5D Mk III
Lens: 16–35mm (at 16mm)
Aperture: f/11
Shutter speed: 1/4 sec.
ISO: 100
Filter(s): 3-stop ND grad

165 THE BIG FOREGROUND
Camera: Nikon D300
Lens: 12–24mm (at 15mm)
Aperture: f/16
Shutter speed: 10 sec.
ISO: 200
Filter(s): 3-stop ND, 2-stop ND grad

167 MINIMALIST SEASCAPE
Camera: Nikon D700
Lens: 17–35mm (at 17mm)
Aperture: f/8
Shutter speed: 163 sec.
ISO: 200
Filter(s): 10-stop ND

167 MINIMALIST MONOCHROME
Camera: Canon EOS 5D Mk II
Lens: 21mm
Aperture: f/16
Shutter speed: 44 sec.
ISO: 100
Filter(s): 4-stop ND

168 IMPRESSIONIST LAKE SCENE
Camera: Nikon F4
Lens: 24–50mm (at 24mm)
Aperture: f/16
Shutter speed: Unrecorded
ISO: 3200 (Fujichrome 1600 film pushed 1 stop)
Filter(s): Diffuser

169 ICM
Camera: Nikon D800E
Lens: 70–200mm (at 200mm)
Aperture: f/16
Shutter speed: 1.3 sec.
ISO: 100
Filter(s): –

170 SEMI-ABSTRACT
Camera: Nikon D300
Lens: 17–50mm (at 50mm)
Aperture: f/14
Shutter speed: 13 sec.
ISO: 100
Filter(s): –

171 REFLECTIONS
Camera: Nikon D200
Lens: 80–400mm (at 400mm)
Aperture: f/5.6
Shutter speed: 1/160 sec.
ISO: 100
Filter(s): –

173 YOUR PERSONAL STYLE
Camera: Canon EOS 5D Mk III
Lens: 24–105mm (at 67mm)
Aperture: f/22
Shutter speed: 15 sec.
ISO: 100
Filter(s): 4-stop ND

174 SUBJECT CHOICE AND EXPOSURE
Camera: Canon EOS 5D Mk III
Lens: 16–35mm (at 18mm)
Aperture: f/16
Shutter speed: 4 sec.
ISO: 100
Filter(s): 4-stop ND grad

175 FRAMING AND LIGHT
Camera: Canon EOS 5D Mk III
Lens: 24–105mm (at 40mm)
Aperture: f/16
Shutter speed: 1/13 sec.
ISO: 100
Filter(s): 2-stop ND grad, polarizer

176 MARK'S PERSONAL STYLE
Camera: Pentax 67II
Lens: 45mm
Aperture: f/22
Shutter speed: Unrecorded
ISO: 50 (Fuji Velvia film)
Filter(s): 3-stop ND grad

179 ROSS'S PERSONAL STYLE
Camera: Nikon D800
Lens: 17–35mm (at 35mm)
Aperture: f/16
Shutter speed: 120 sec.
ISO: 200
Filter(s): 2-stop ND grad

USEFUL WEBSITES AND DOWNLOADS

CALIBRATION

ColorEyes Display:

www.integrated-color.com

ColorVision: www.colorvision.com

Xrite: www.xrite.com

CAMERA CARE

Giottos: www.giottos.com

Visible Dust: www.visibledust.com

DEPTH-OF-FIELD CALCULATOR

DOF Master: www.dofmaster.com

OUTDOOR EQUIPMENT

Ordnance Survey:

www.ordnancesurvey.co.uk

Paramo: www.paramo.co.uk

SatMap: www.satmap.com

PHOTOGRAPHERS

Mark Bauer:

www.markbauerphotography.com

Ross Hoddinott:

www.rosshoddinott.co.uk

PHOTOGRAPHIC EQUIPMENT

Canon: www.canon.com

Cokin: www.cokin.com

Fstop gear: www.fstopgear.com

Fujifilm: www.fujifilm.com

Gitzo: www.gitzo.com

Lee Filters: www.leefilters.com

Lexar: www.lexar.com

Manfrotto: www.manfrotto.com

Nikon: www.nikon.com

Olympus: www.olympus.com

Pentax: www.pentaximaging.com

Really Right Stuff:

www.reallyrightstuff.com

Sigma: www.sigma-photo.com

Sony: www.sony.com

Tamron: www.tamron.com

PHOTOGRAPHY WORKSHOPS

Dawn 2 Dusk Photography:

www.dawn2duskphotography.com

PLANNING

The Photographer's Ephemeris:

www.photoephemeris.com

PhotoPills: www.photopills.com

SOFTWARE

Adobe: www.adobe.com

Apple: www.apple.com/aperture

GIMP: www.gimp.org

Neat Image: www.neatimage.com

Nik Software: www.niksoftware.com

Noiseware: www.imagenomic.com

Photomatix Pro: www.hdrsoft.com

Pixel Genius: www.pixelgenius.com

RawTherapee: www.rawtherapee.com

WEATHER

AccuWeather: www.accuweather.com

Metcheck: www.metcheck.com

The Met office: www.metoffice.gov.uk

XC Weather: www.xcweather.co.uk

Yr: www.yr.no

TIDE TIMES

Tide-Forecast: www.tide-forecast.com

GLOSSARY

Angle of view The area of a scene that a lens takes in, measured in degrees.

Aspect ratio The relative horizontal and vertical measurements. For example, if an image has an aspect ratio of 2:1, it means that the width is twice the length of the height.

Aperture The opening in a camera lens through which light passes to expose the image sensor. The relative size of the aperture is denoted by f/numbers.

Autofocus (AF) A through-the-lens focusing system that allows accurate focus without the user manually focusing the lens.

Camera shake Movement of the camera during exposure that, particularly at slow shutter speeds, can lead to blurred images. Often caused by handholding the camera or an unsteady support.

Colour temperature The colour of a light source expressed in degrees Kelvin (K).

Composition The placement or arrangement of visual elements. The term composition means 'putting together' and can apply to any work of art. It is a term often used interchangeably with design, form or visual ordering.

Context In composition, context refers to surroundings and placing objects so that they remain in keeping with their environment.

Contrast The range between the highlight and shadow areas of an image, or a marked difference in illumination between colours or adjacent areas.

Cropping To remove part of the image, usually in order to enhance the composition or balance.

Depth of field (DOF) The amount of an image that appears acceptably sharp. This is primarily controlled by the aperture setting: the smaller the aperture, the greater the depth of field.

Distortion Typically, when straight lines are not rendered perfectly straight in a photograph. Barrel and pincushion distortion are example of types of lens distortion.

Dynamic range The ability of the camera's sensor to capture a full range of shadows and highlights.

Electronic viewfinder (EVF) A type of viewfinder where the image seen by the lens is projected electronically.

Exposure The amount of light allowed to strike and expose the image sensor, as controlled by the aperture, shutter speed and ISO sensitivity. Also the act of taking a photograph, as in 'making an exposure'.

Exposure compensation A control that allows intentional over- or underexposure.

Filter A piece of coloured, or coated, glass or plastic placed in front of the lens for creative or corrective use.

Focal length The distance, usually in millimetres, from the optical centre of a lens to its focal point, which signifies its power.

Frame To arrange or compose. Also, purposefully using objects within the landscape to create a 'frame', or frame other elements.

F-stop / f-number Number assigned to a particular lens aperture. Wide apertures are denoted by small numbers (such as f/2.8) and small apertures by large numbers (such as f/22).

Grad Graduated filter. A filter that is half-coated, half-clear.

Highlights The brightest areas of an image.

Histogram A graph used to represent the distribution of tones in an image.

ISO (International Standards Organization) The sensitivity of the image sensor measured in terms equivalent to the ISO rating of a film.

JPEG (Joint Photographic Experts Group) A popular image file type, compressed to reduce file size.

Landscape The visible features of an area of land, including the physical elements of landforms and water bodies, such as rivers, lakes and the sea. Also, human elements, including buildings and structures, and transitory elements such as lighting and weather conditions.

LCD (Liquid Crystal Display) The flat screen on the back of a digital camera that allows the user to playback and review digital images and shooting information.

Lens The eye of the camera. The lens projects the image it sees onto the camera's imaging sensor. The size of the lens is measured and indicated as focal length.

Manual focus When focus is achieved through manual rotation of the lens's focusing ring.

Metering Using a camera or handheld lightmeter to determine the amount of light coming from a scene or falling on to it, in order to calculate the required exposure.

Metering pattern The system used by the camera to calculate the exposure.

Megapixel One million pixels equals one megapixel.

Mirror lock-up Allows the reflex mirror of an SLR to be raised and held in the 'up' position, before the exposure is made.

Monochrome Image compromising only of grey tones, from black to white.

Multiplication factor The amount the focal length of a lens will be magnified when attached to a camera with a cropped type sensor.

Negative space The empty space surrounding the main subject in your photo – the subject itself is known as 'positive space'.

Noise Coloured image interference caused by stray electrical signals.

Overexposure A condition when too much light reaches the sensor. Images appear overly bright and detail is lost in the highlights.

Perspective In context of visual perception, it is the way in which objects appear to the eye depending on their spatial attributes, or their dimensions and the position of the eye relative to the objects.

Photoshop A graphics editing program developed and published by Adobe Systems Incorporated. It is considered the industry standard for editing and processing photographs.

Pixel Abbreviation of 'picture element'. Pixels are the smallest bits of information that combine to form a digital image.

Post-processing The use of software to make adjustments to a digital file on a computer.

Prime A lens with a fixed focal length lens.

RAW A versatile and widely used digital file format whereby the shooting parameters are attached to the file, rather than embedded within it, enabling them to be reversed and edited without a loss of image quality.

Remote release A device used to trigger the shutter of a tripod-mounted camera to avoid camera shake.

Resolution The number of pixels used to capture an image or display it, usually expressed in ppi. The higher the resolution, the finer the detail.

RGB (Red, Green, Blue) Computers and other digital devices understand colour information as shades of red, green and blue.

Rule of thirds A compositional device that places the key elements of a picture at points along imagined lines that divide the frame into thirds.

Saturation The intensity of the colours in an image.

Shadow areas The darkest areas of a scene.

Silhouette The dark shape or outline of an (underexposed) object cast against a brighter background.

Shutter The mechanism that controls the amount of light reaching the sensor by opening and closing.

Shutter speed The length of time the sensor is exposed to light; shutter speed determines the duration of an exposure.

SLR (Single Lens Reflex) A camera type that allows the user to view the scene through the lens, using a reflex mirror.

Spot metering A metering system that places importance on the intensity of light reflected by a very small percentage of the frame.

Standard lens A focal length similar to the vision of the human eye. 50mm is considered a standard lens on a 35mm / full frame camera.

Symmetry Corresponding in size, form and arrangement on the opposite side of a plane, line or point. Regularity of form or arrangement.

Telephoto lens A lens with a large focal length and a narrow angle of view

TIFF (Tagged Image File Format) A universal file format supported by virtually all image-editing applications. TIFFS are uncompressed digital files.

TTL (Through-The-Lens) metering A metering system built into the camera that measures light passing through the lens at the time of shooting.

Underexposure A condition in which too little light reaches the sensor. The resulting image will be dark, possibly resulting in a loss of detail in the shadow areas.

Vanishing point The point at which parallel lines appear to converge in the rendering of perspective – often on the horizon.

Viewfinder An optical system used for composing and sometimes focusing the subject. Also known as OVF (optical viewfinder) to differentiate it from an EVF.

Vignetting Darkening of the corners of an image caused either by the design of the lens (optical vignetting) or the use of the incorrect lens hood and / or multiple stacked filters (mechanical vignetting).

White balance A function that allows the correct colour balance to be recorded for any given lighting situation.

Wide-angle lens A lens with a short focal length that delivers a wide angle of view.

Zoom A lens that covers a range of focal lengths.

ABOUT THE AUTHORS

MARK BAUER

Mark Bauer is a leading landscape photographer and technical writer. He is renowned for his evocative, intimate images of the south-west of England. Mark's work is featured in *Landscape Photography Magazine*, *Digital Photographer* and similar publications. He is a contributor to three leading picture libraries and he has had a number of competition successes in the Landscape Photographer of the Year, Outdoor Photographer of the Year and International Garden Photographer of the Year competitions. He also one of Manfrotto's 'Local Heroes'.

The Art of Landscape Photography is Mark's fourth book and follows on from *The Landscape Photography Workshop*, which is also published by GMC Publications. He co-runs Dawn 2 Dusk Photography with Ross Hoddinott. To find out more about Mark and his work, visit www.markbauerphotography.com.

ROSS HODDINOTT

Ross Hoddinott is one of the UK's leading professional outdoor photographers. He is a regular contributor to a number of photographic publications, including *Digital SLR Photography* and *Wild Planet* magazine. He is a multi-award winner, having won the British Wildlife Photographer of the Year competition in 2009, and been commended in the Wildlife Photographer of the Year, International Garden Photographer of the Year and Landscape Photographer of the Year competitions. He is an Ambassador for Nikon UK, a Manfrotto 'Local Hero', and was a member of the 2020VISION photo-team – the largest, most ambitious multimedia conservation project ever staged in the UK.

The Art of Landscape Photography is Ross's eighth photography book. Previous titles include, *The Digital Exposure Handbook* and *The Landscape Photography Workshop*. Together with Mark Bauer, Ross runs Dawn 2 Dusk Photography, specializing in landscape photography workshops in the UK. Find out more about Ross at www.rosshoddinott.co.uk.

ACKNOWLEDGEMENTS

Thank you to everyone at GMC Publications for helping compile this book. Particular thanks go to Jonathan Bailey, Gerrie Purcell, Dominique Page, Chris Gatcum and Simon Goggin. Thank you also to Canon, Lee Filters, Manfrotto, Nikon, Phase One and Really Right Stuff for supplying suitable product images.

However, as you might expect, the biggest 'thank you' is reserved for our long-suffering families – Mark's wife Julie and son Harry; and Ross's wife Fliss and children Evie, Maya and Jude. Quite simply, photographers are a nightmare to live with! The hours are long, unsociable and unpredictable. Photographers tend to be a moody bunch – often grumpy when the weather isn't playing ball or when a deadline is fast approaching. Thank you for putting up with us and for your unwavering support, encouragement, patience and belief.

Finally, a big thank you to all our workshop participants, who have encouraged us to share our knowledge and experience to an even wider audience through this book and our previous title, *The Landscape Photography Workshop*. If you haven't attended one of our Dawn 2 Dusk Photography Workshops yet, we hope you can join us soon…

INDEX

To order a book, or to request a catalogue, contact:

Ammonite Press

AE Publications Ltd, 166 High Street, Lewes,

East Sussex, BN7 1XU United Kingdom

Tel: +44 (0)1273 488006

www.ammonitepress.com